S0-BCT-210

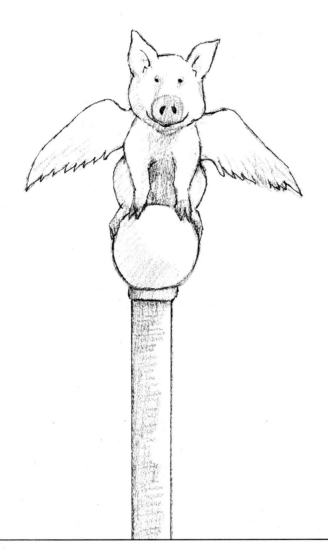

PERFECT THE PIG

by Susan Jeschke

Holt, Rinehart and Winston / New York

To my mother,
Victoria Kochman Newmark

Copyright © 1981 by Susan Jeschke All rights reserved, including the
right to reproduce this book or portions thereof in any form. Published
simultaneously in Canada by Holt, Rinehart and Winston of Canada, Limited.

He was so small that his mother didn't know he was there. The other piglets were always pushing and shoving, squealing greedily for food, or rolling around in the mud.

But the tiny pig was gentle, quiet, and never greedy, and he always kept clean.

While the other piglets played he would lie under his favorite tree wishing for wings to carry him into the sky.

One day he heard a great shriek. A large sow had slipped on the road. The little pig crawled under the fence and ran to help her.

He wedged some pebbles and twigs under her, and with great effort finally helped her to her feet.

The sow was very grateful and offered the little pig a wish—"anything at all," she said.

"I want wings," he answered.

The sow nodded and continued on her way. Almost at once wings began to grow on the little pig.

He was thrilled. His wings worked! He flew around all day.

At night he returned to the pigpen. When the other pigs saw his wings they pushed him out. "Go sleep with the birds," they said.

He tried that, but the birds
wouldn't let him stay either.

On and on he flew towards a city.

He landed on a fire escape, too tired and hungry to go
on. A woman came to the window. "So tiny, and with
such beautiful wings. How perfect!" she said, lifting him
inside.

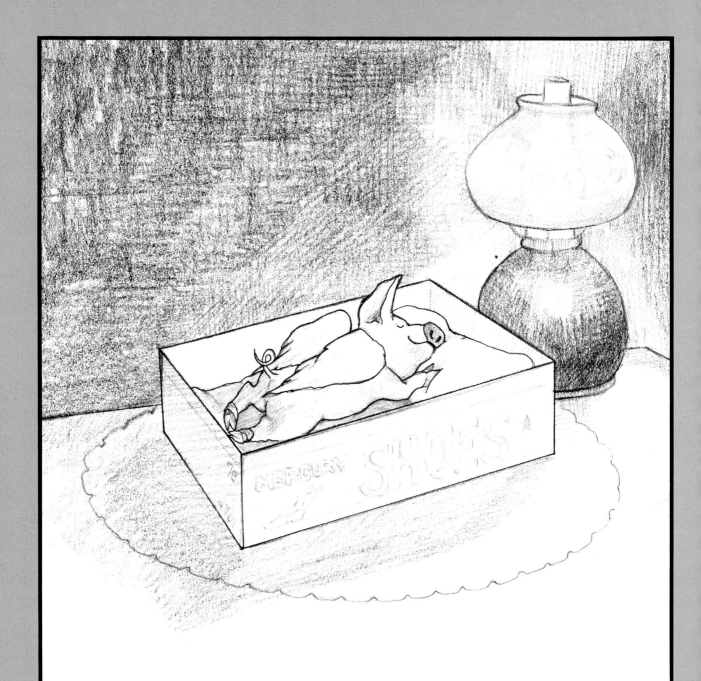

She fed him, then put him to bed and kissed him goodnight. The little pig kissed her back. This so delighted the woman that she named the pig "Perfect." Perfect could hardly believe it. He had not only found a home, but someone who thought he was perfect.

Olive—that was the woman's name—was an artist. She adored Perfect and did all she could to please him. She bathed him . . .

. . . and fed him the choicest vegetables, some of which she grew in the apartment.

Soon she began to make pictures of Perfect posed
among fruits and vegetables. He was a wonderful
model.

However, he soon grew restless
and looked longingly at the sky.
Olive understood and took him up to the roof.

He flew about while she waited for him.

Olive made a little jacket to cover Perfect's wings so he wouldn't attract attention when she took him on walks.

But Perfect didn't like walking. The cement hurt his feet, and he couldn't see anything. So Olive carried him in her basket.

She tried her best to shelter him from the harsh things in life, but she didn't always succeed.

Whole Pigs
ALL SIZES

People liked the pictures of
Perfect and bought them.
Olive's savings jar began to fill up.

Soon the apartment was crowded with pictures, fruits
and vegetables, and a growing Perfect. By now he had
grown so much that he was getting too big to hide.

Olive decided that the best thing for both of them would be to live in the country. She pasted a label on her savings jar. It said HOUSE IN THE COUNTRY.
Perfect couldn't read, but he could see that Olive was very happy and excited. That made him happy and excited too.

But their happiness did not last long. The next day, while Perfect was out for his daily fly, a heavy fog rolled in. Perfect got lost. He flew around frantically as it grew darker and darker.

When the fog lifted, Perfect spotted a park bench. He landed on it and fell sound asleep. A man's gravelly voice woke him. "Well, I'll be—a pig with wings! My fortune is made!" the man said.

He picked Perfect up and ran home with him.

Perfect found himself in a small room. The man took off his belt and said, "okay, Oink. Now I'm going to train you. Fly around this room!" He cracked the belt, and Perfect flew away from it in fright. "That's a good Oink," the man said.

Then he emptied his garbage and gave it to Perfect to eat. Perfect was shocked and ran to the window.

"Oh, no you don't," the man said, and tied Perfect to a pipe.

When the man was satisfied with the training he bought
Perfect a costume and took him to a park to perform.

At the end of the performance
Perfect would fly over the heads
of the audience.
Everyone oohed and ahhed
and the man collected lots of money.

Every night, after counting the money, the man gave Perfect a hard look and tied him up tighter. Once Perfect tried to resist and flapped his wings. "Trying to fly away, eh? I'll fix you, you flying porkchop," the man said.

He left the room and returned with a cage. From then on that was where Perfect was kept.

Perfect was miserable. His wings ached and he hadn't had a bath in months. The man gave him only garbage to eat and never ever kissed him. Every night Perfect cried himself to sleep thinking of Olive.

Olive went up to the roof each day and searched the sky for Perfect. She wandered through the streets looking for him.

Sometimes she wondered if Perfect had been a dream.
The one remaining picture of him reminded her that he
was real.

During one of her daily walks, she saw a sign that read THE GREAT FLYING OINK. Olive immediately bought a ticket and went in.

She could hardly believe her eyes. It was Perfect! The man leaning over him was saying, "Fly, you stupid Oink—or it's off to the butcher with you!" But Perfect couldn't budge. He was so sad, and his wings hurt.

"Perfect!" Olive cried out. Perfect raised his head. He squealed as he stretched his wings and flew to her. Everyone clapped.

Olive took off the leash. "Where are you going with my pig, lady?" the man said. "This is *my* pig," said Olive. The man and Olive began to argue. "Let a judge decide this," someone said. Everyone agreed.

The judge listened to both sides. First the man spoke, then Olive. The judge thought hard. Then he said, "let the pig choose!" Perfect, of course, chose Olive. The judge also awarded Olive half the man's earnings, which, he said, was Perfect's rightful share.

With the money, Olive bought a little house in the country, where she and Perfect lived in peace and happiness.

The End

Behind the Scenes

Fun-To-Do Activities Begin on Page 54

Behind the Scenes

Introduction

Birds were not the first animals to fly. Their *ancestors* (parents, grandparents and so on) were the dinosaurs, and some dinosaurs could fly, long before Perfect in *Perfect the Pig* knew how.

Great Flying Lizards

Dinosaurs were the great animals that roamed the earth millions of years ago. There were many different kinds of dinosaurs. Some were ferocious, like the *Tyrannosaurus*. This dinosaur ate meat and could grow as tall as a two-story house. Some dinosaurs were quiet and peaceful, like the *Apatasaurus*. This dinosaur ate only plants, but it ate a lot of them. It grew as long as two school buses. And some dinosaurs, like the *Archaeopteryx,* could fly.

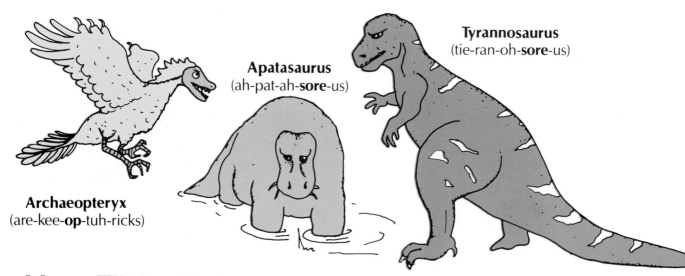

Tyrannosaurus
(tie-ran-oh-**sore**-us)

Apatasaurus
(ah-pat-ah-**sore**-us)

Archaeopteryx
(are-kee-**op**-tuh-ricks)

How Flight Began

Early dinosaurs walked on short, stubby legs. They looked like today's alligators and crocodiles. Some dinosaurs eventually grew longer legs.

42

With longer legs, they could move more quickly, find food more easily and escape their enemies better. Soon some dinosaurs with longer, thinner legs learned how to leap. Leaping worked even better for catching food. Longer and longer leaps *evolved* — or developed over time — into flight.

The First Bird

The first bird was called *Archaeopteryx* (say: are-kee-**op**-tuh-ricks). That means "ancient wing." Scientists first found traces of it in Germany. It was about the size of a pigeon. The front legs of this little dinosaur had evolved into wings. And the dinosaur scales had become longer and lighter. The dinosaur that came just before it had scales only on its head and feet; the rest of its body was covered with feathers. Archaeopteryx, however, had feathers all over.

Fine Feathers

Dinosaurs were *reptiles*. Alligators, lizards and snakes are the reptiles we know today. All reptiles are *cold-blooded*. This means that their bodies are the same temperature as the air around them.

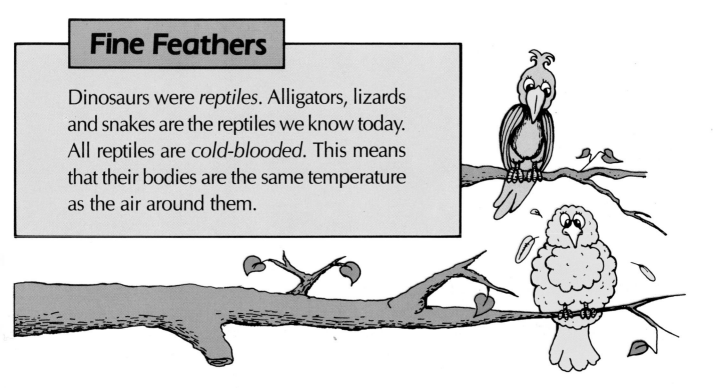

Behind the Scenes

When it is cold at night, reptiles cool off. In fact, they get so cold that they can hardly move. In extreme heat, they cannot move either. But when they developed feathers, these early birds did not get too cold or overheat. They could fluff up their feathers to trap a layer of warm air next to their bodies, to protect themselves from the cold. And to protect themselves from the heat, they could open their feathers, allowing the heat from their bodies to escape. Scientists believe that the dinosaurs disappeared when the weather became too cold for them to survive. But the birds, with the help of their feathers, lived on.

How It Began

Scientists think that the ancestors of Archaeopteryx lived in trees. They may have started flying by gliding from branch to branch. Archaeopteryx had longer, stronger wings than today's birds. Gliding took it from high in a tree to the ground. It could catch insects in the air. But once on the ground, it could not fly up again. It had to use the claws on the ends of its wings to crawl up to a high place again.

Birds Today

Birds have come a long way since then. They come in all shapes and sizes. They live everywhere on the earth. But all have feathers that used to be scales, and wings that used to be front legs.

EVOLUTION: Some creatures changed over millions of years into the animals and birds we know today. This change over a long period of time is called *evolution.*

How Frogs Grow

Some animals change, or evolve, over a long period of time. Other animals change more quickly. They can change their whole bodies within the span of their lives. This change is called *metamorphosis* (say: met-ah-**more**-fuh-sis).

One animal that changes through metamorphosis is the frog. The frog is an *amphibian*. An amphibian is an animal that lives in the water and on the land during different stages of its life. Toads and salamanders are amphibians, too.

A frog's life begins in the water. A female frog lays eggs in a pond or stream. These eggs float on the surface of the water. Each egg grows into a tadpole in about two weeks. A tadpole looks like a little black fish with a tail.

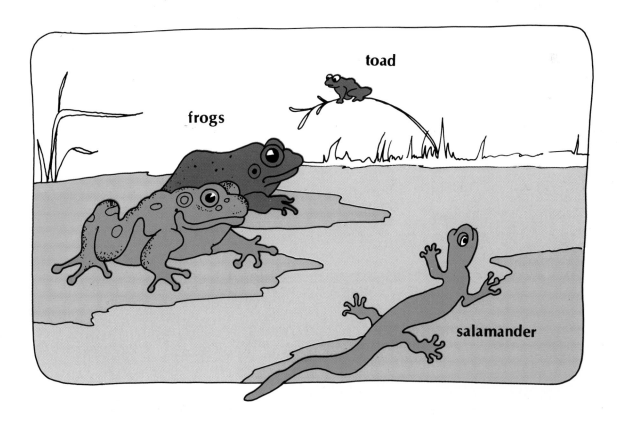

Behind the Scenes

Inside The Tadpole

The tadpole takes oxygen from the water through gills. Within two weeks, the tadpole's gills begin to close. The back legs of the frog begin to appear three weeks later. When the tadpole is eight weeks old, it is breathing air through lungs. Now the tadpole has to come to the surface of the water to take gulps of air. The gills have disappeared.

gills

More Changes

The tadpole's body now begins to change on the outside. First the tail grows shorter. Then the back legs grow stronger. Front legs are the last to appear. The whole metamorphosis takes about fourteen weeks from tadpole to frog. If you live near a pond, it's a real treat to watch this wonder of nature each spring.

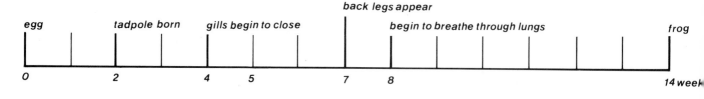

Kites Through The Ages

Kites were invented 2,000 years ago in China. Over the years, they have been used as toys and more. They were used to raise weather instruments up into the clouds. And they were also used to study how things fly. From these experiments, people learned how to build the first gliders and airplanes.

Behind the Scenes

Benjamin Franklin, who lived in Philadelphia in the 1700s, did a kite experiment that answered many questions about electricity. He flew a kite during a thunderstorm. Electricity traveled down the wet kite string and to a brass key, and sparks jumped from the key to Franklin's hand. It was a dangerous way to learn how electricity works. Franklin risked his life for science and won.

The Wright brothers—Orville and Wilbur—built the first successful airplane which they flew at Kitty Hawk, North Carolina, in 1903. The Wright brothers used the shape of a box kite to build their first *glider*. A glider is an airplane without a motor. It glides on air currents much the same way a kite does.

Behind the Scenes

Flying For Fun

To many people a breezy day means only one thing—kite weather. Flying a kite is great fun. A kite flies on the wind. It dips, dives and soars like something alive—like a bird. You can control a kite with a long string tied to its center. With this string, you can make a kite fly and dance through the air.

Here A Pig, There A Pig

If you have visited a farm, perhaps your favorite animal is one you saw there. Horses? Cows? Sheep?

Or chickens? Did you know that chickens are the most common animal found on a farm? Half of all farmers in this country keep chickens. Some raise egg-laying hens, others raise chickens for food.

And did you know that one of the most difficult animals to raise is a pig? If you keep a herd of pigs, most of your energy will go into feeding them.

It takes two tons (4,000 pounds) of feed to feed 350 pigs for three days. As the saying goes, "they eat like pigs!"

Pigs eat a lot of shelled corn. Pig farmers grind the corn in a mill and then mix it with a protein *supplement* (something added to make the food whole and healthy). The pigs and *hogs* (hogs are pigs that weigh over 120 pounds) live in three separate places, grouped by size. The farmer keeps busy filling all three bins. Pigs don't get excited when they see the farmer bringing food because the food bins, called *troughs,* are never empty.

Mother pigs, called *sows,* live separately from the rest of the pigs. Sows eat grass, clover and alfalfa instead of corn. A sow will have a *litter* of six to nine baby pigs, or *piglets.* Sows stay with their litters in a kind of pig nursery, a barn called a *farrowing house,* for six weeks. At the end of each day, the farmer must clean out the farrowing house and spread a fresh layer of straw bedding for the pigs.

Pig farmers have to perform minor surgery on the baby pigs. At birth, pigs have eight sharp teeth called "needle teeth." The farmer cuts these off, to protect the other pigs from the danger of a sharp bite. Tails are removed, also.

When hogs have "pigged" their way up to 220 pounds, they are shipped off to market to be sold. Then, the pig farmer starts all over again.

Behind the Scenes

Your Pet's Health

Owning a pet can be a lot of fun. But there is a serious side to having a pet too. In addition to love, your pet will depend on you for many things—food, water, exercise and health care. The first things are easier to take care of than your pet's health. What do you do when your pet is sick?

There are doctors who only have animal patients. These doctors are called *veterinarians*. If you do not know a vet before you buy a pet, find one soon after you bring your pet home. There are many things a veterinarian can do to keep your puppy, kitten or other pet healthy. Some veterinarians treat many animals—hamsters, rabbits and birds, too. Find a vet who's right for your pet.

When you take your new pet to the doctor, your pet will be examined. Sometimes an animal has a birth defect that you should know about. For example, a dog may be born deaf or a kitten may have a crooked spine. If you can, you should take an animal to a vet before you buy it. This way, you'll know if the animal will need special care. Some pet stores not only allow this, but encourage it. After all, a happy pet owner will return to the pet store again.

On your pet's first visit, the doctor will listen to your puppy's or kitten's heart and lungs with a stethoscope — just like your doctor does with you. Then the vet will check your pet's teeth. A healthy young animal's teeth should grow in straight. The ears will be checked for mites. Mites and fleas are tiny insects that can cause infections on your pet's skin and in the ears. Puppies receive shots to protect them from three serious diseases that dogs can catch. Kittens get one shot to keep them safe from disease.

After the checkup, the doctor will talk to you about what to feed your pet. The vet will also let you know how much exercise your pet needs. If your pet needs vitamins, the doctor will tell you which vitamins are needed and how to give them to your pet.

The veterinarian will keep a file on your pet. When you go to see the doctor again, the vet will already know a lot about your pet, the patient. It is good to take your pet for a checkup once a year. A healthy pet is a happy pet.

Behind the Scenes

Why Paint?

A painter is an artist who expresses feelings in paint. Happy feelings look different in a picture than sad feelings do. But how does this happen?

There are many things that go into painting a picture. Let's look at some of them.

Color is one thing. Bright colors look happier than dark colors. Using yellow in your painting expresses a different feeling than using brown does.

Form is another. Are there many straight lines in your picture? Or are there more wiggly ones? Straight lines give a feeling of calmness and order. Wiggly and curly lines can look restless or lively — they add action to a painting.

Think about *composition*. Composition means the way you choose to arrange the people or things in your picture. Is one person close to another in your picture? Close to a plant? Perhaps you fill your whole picture with things close together. Or you choose to paint only one thing to fill up the whole space. Each way you can compose a picture gives it a different feeling.

A painter has certain tools to work with. Paint, of course. And brushes. *Canvas* to paint on, too. Canvas is a certain kind of cloth that absorbs paint well. The canvas is framed on wood, and then it is propped on a stand called an *easel* when the painter is painting.

Art museums are wonderful places to visit. You will find many examples of different kinds of paintings. Some museums have special programs for children who want to learn more about painting or who want to try painting pictures themselves.

Why not try your hand at painting? After all, there is no right or wrong in painting—it's a matter of what you see and how you see it.

Activities ➡

Activities

Leaf Painting

Every leaf has a beautiful design. Bring out its beauty and keep it forever in a leaf print. Here's how.

You'll need this equipment:

—a brush   —some watercolors   —newspapers
—a jar of water   —library paste   —construction paper

- Choose the leaves you want to print. Leave them pressed in a book for at least a week.
- Put a little paste on a dish.
- Add a little water to the colors you want to use.
- Cut newspaper into sheets 6″ by 8″.
- Place a leaf on one piece of the newspaper.
- Dip your brush in water, then into the library paste. Apply the paste to the leaf.
- Rinse the brush.
- Tip the brush in color and apply it to the leaf over the paste.
- Place the leaf on construction paper, painted side down.

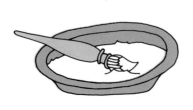

- Put a clean strip of newspaper over the leaf, hold the leaf in place by the stem and rub over the leaf gently with your thumb or one finger.
- Lift up the top piece of the newspaper and the leaf to see the print.

You can put two or three colors on the leaf, but be sure to rinse the brush well between colors. Just follow these step-by-step instructions, and you'll have beautiful leaf prints to hang on the wall or give as gifts!

Trivia Game

Trivia are facts that may be unimportant but are very interesting. You can make up a game using trivia. Here are some to start you off. Put them on cards. Write the question on one side and the answer on the other. Stump your friends.

1. Q. What animals were the first to fly in a man-made machine?
   A. A rooster, a duck and a sheep flew over Paris in 1792 in a hot air balloon.
2. Q. Which are stronger, people or elephants?
   A. People. In a tug of war between a 6,000 pound elephant and 50 men weighing a total of 6,000 pounds, the men won.
3. Q. Which is bigger, a blue whale or an elephant?
   A. A blue whale is the largest creature on earth. The blue whale weighs about the same as 20 elephants!

Activities

Lost And Found

These animal mothers have lost their animal babies. Help them get back together again. Match the animal mother picture below to the description, or word picture, of her animal baby.

Description

Lost — one fluffy ball of fur that cries like a baby — "mew"

Lost — a tiny black amphibian that starts changing its form as soon as it's born

Lost — one smart little underwater animal that must be pushed to the surface for its first breath

Lost — one long-legged animal with soft beautiful eyes that gets up and runs within hours of its birth — "neigh"

Lost — one scrawny, bare-skinned creature that breaks out of an egg before it learns to fly

Animal Mother

Crazy Pictures

A collage is a picture made with just about anything under the sun. Pieces of fabric, buttons, straws, leaves, feathers, colored paper and newspaper are only a few of the things you can use. Glue the collage pieces on heavy paper or cardboard. You can be neat, or you can overlap the pieces of your collage in a wild way. You can paint your collage pieces, or you can paint around them. Keep a collection of collage materials in a shoe box. Add things to the box that interest you when you find them. Follow these steps to make a tissue paper collage.

1. Cut or tear colored tissue paper into small pieces.
2. Brush glue all over a piece of heavy paper or cardboard.
3. Put the tissue on the cardboard and press down.
4. Repeat with different colors of tissue until the cardboard is covered. Try doing more layers the same way, adding more glue where you want to put more tissue paper.
5. After you've added all the tissue you want, you can brush glue over the whole picture. This crinkles the design and makes the colors run together in an interesting way.
6. Let your collage dry. Then hang it on the wall or place it on a window sill to catch the sunlight—and see how pretty the colors are.

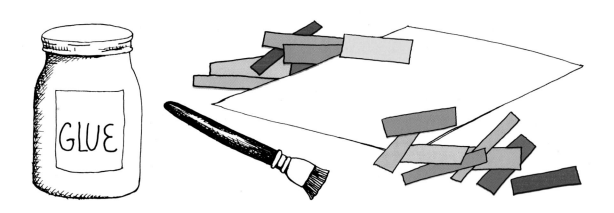

Activities

Fly In Style

Do you like paper airplanes? How about paper spaceships, or other fancy fliers? Trace this flying ship, then color in stripes and numbers to make your paper airplane super special.

1. Trace the black lines of the jet, then cut out around the edges of your tracing. Then color it in.
2. Fold *up* on line A.
3. Fold *down* on lines B.
4. Fold *up* on lines C.
5. Have fun flying your jet.

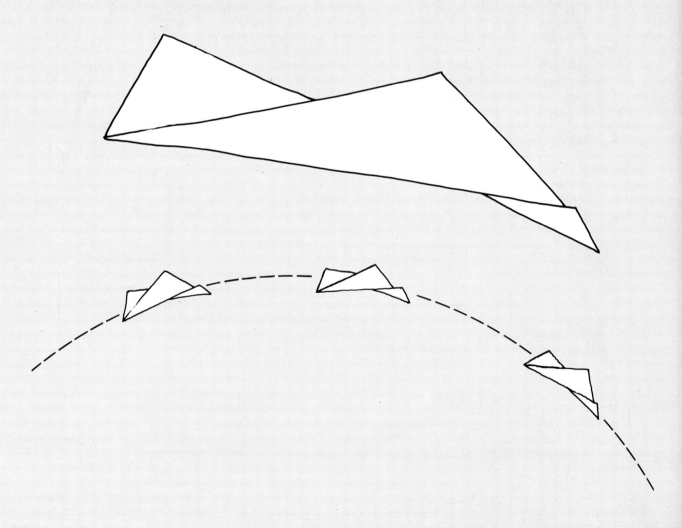

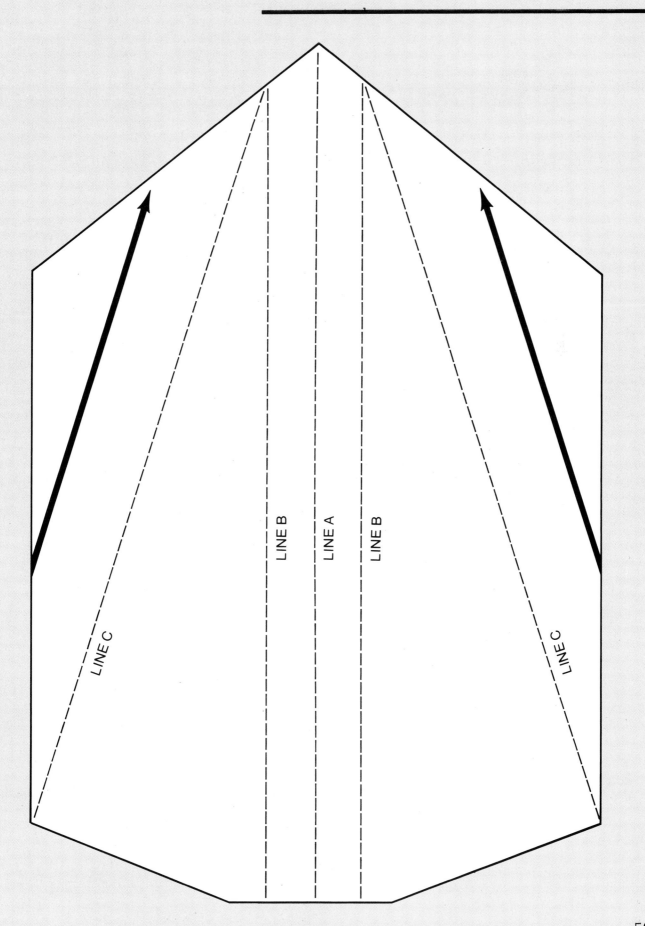

LINE C

LINE B

LINE A

LINE B

LINE C

Activities

Did You Know...?

- The guinea pig and the ground hog are not related to pigs at all. They are both rodents.

- The prehistoric bird called the elephant bird laid eggs that were approximately 30 times larger than a chicken's egg.

- Orville Wright, the first person ever to fly, lived to see Neil Armstrong become the first person to set foot on the moon.

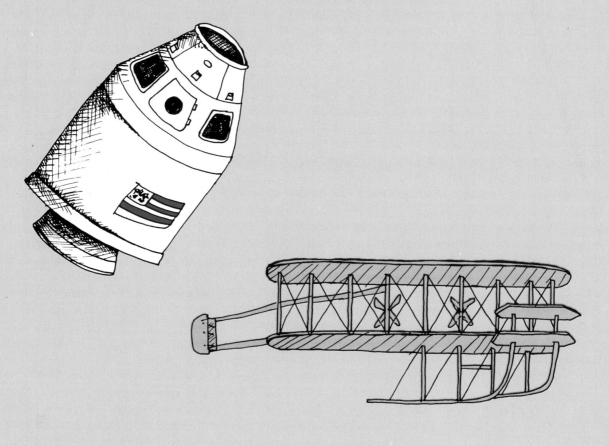

Word Search

Hidden in the maze below are words you've just learned.

Do you remember what they mean? The words go across and down. Find the words in the maze, then write them on another paper.

REPTILE, HOG, AMPHIBIAN, LARVA, TADPOLE, SOW, CANVAS, KITE, LIZARD, EASEL

C	H	R	N	S	X	L	T	S	T
A	R	E	P	T	I	L	E	T	A
N	L	I	Z	A	R	D	K	R	D
V	X	A	J	B	L	S	I	L	P
A	C	S	T	Y	A	B	T	E	O
S	H	O	G	D	R	M	E	K	L
P	Z	W	U	H	V	M	A	G	E
L	Q	F	N	E	A	S	E	L	C
P	G	N	R	G	W	Y	L	S	P
A	M	P	H	I	B	I	A	N	W

Activities

What Do You See?

Is this a funny face or a basket of fruit? What do you see? An ink blot like this tests your imagination.

Your imagination is a key to seeing the world in new ways. Look up at the clouds. Do you see horses running, boats sailing, and misty mountains in the sky? If you don't, lie back and look at clouds again. This time use your imagination.

Jokes

Q. What days are the strongest?
A. Saturdays and Sundays, because all the other days are "weak" days.

Little Kid: "I'd like to buy a puppy, sir. How much do they cost?"
Store Owner: "Ten dollars apiece."
Little Kid: "How much does a whole one cost?"

Betty: "I know a man who was put in jail
        for stealing a pig."
 Sam: "How did they catch him?"
Betty: "The pig squealed."

Hide And Seek

Big cities are crowded and busy. Even the sky is filled with activity over the city. How many of the following flying things can you spot in this picture?

bird, helicopter, kite, butterfly, leaf

Activities

Do-It-Yourself Bank

Homemade banks began as kitchen pots made of an Irish clay called pyg. When the Irish told English manufacturers that they wanted *pyg* pots, the English thought they meant *pig* pots and made pots shaped like pigs. These two sound-alike words gave us the small, home coin holders we call piggy banks.

You can make your own piggy bank out of a small tissue box.

1. Cut five pieces of construction paper the size of the four sides and top of an empty tissue box. (Hint: you can trace the sides on construction paper to get the size just right.)
2. Paste the pieces of construction paper on the sides and top of the box.
3. With the tip of your scissors, cut a hole in the top where the tissue box opening is.
4. Draw or paint a family of pigs around the sides, or add a collage. Make it festive, then save your pennies and see how quickly they add up.